# Totally Twins
## Birthday Bonanza

The Fabulous Diary
of Persephone Pinchgut

Sweet Cherry
Publishing

Author
Aleesah Darlison

Illustrator
Serena Geddes

Published by Sweet Cherry Publishing Limited
Unit E, Vulcan Business Complex
Vulcan Road
Leicester, LE5 3EB
United Kingdom

www.sweetcherrypublishing.com

First published in the UK in 2016
ISBN: 978-1-78226-298-5

Published by Sweet Cherry Publishing in 2016

First published in Australia in 2010 by
New Frontier Publishing

Birthday Bonanza: The Fabulous Diary of Persephone Pinchgut

Series: Darlison, Aleesah. Totally twins.
Target Audience: For primary school age.
Other Authors/Contributors:
Geddes, Serena.

Designed by Nicholas Pike

Printed and bound in India by Thomson Press India Ltd.

*To Hayley and Jasmine,*
*two of my greatest fans.*
*Aleesah Darlison*

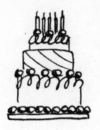

*For Molly and Chloe, who are both*
*effortlessly cool and totally awesome.*
*Love Serena*

## Monday 3 May. 3:42 pm.

In the kitchen, scoffing home-made caramel cookies.

Hi, and welcome to my fourth fabulous diary. I can't believe I've managed to fill three diaries already.

In less than three months.

**WOW.**

Who would have thought I'd have so many amazing things to write down?

BTW (by the way), you simply must read my other diaries. They're meant to be **TOP SECRET**, but I think I'll let you read them. They're too good not to share. So, when you've finished this diary go back and read the others – if you haven't already. If you dare!

As you can probably tell by the time, I've just got home from school. Today is the first day of term. It was a struggle getting out of bed this morning because Portia and I only arrived home from Fiji last night.

Portia is my pet crocodile. Teehee! Not really. She is actually my identical twin sister, which can sometimes be the same as having a pet crocodile, especially when she is tired and snippety-snappety like she was this morning when we had to get

up for school. I'm the cool sister, BTW.

We really missed Mum while we were away and didn't have much time to chat to her when we got home late last night. Mum was keen to get us 'back into our routine' and off to school this morning. I think she might have TOP SECRET business of her own to attend to at the moment. She seems rather distracted. I will have to get to the bottom of it.

However, I have DIGRESSED, which is a word I learned today from my new teacher, Miss Squirrel-Smith. It means I'm going off on a different tack to the one I should be on.

Miss Squirrel-Smith has replaced our old teacher, Mr Cleaver. (Well, he's not that old, just on the wrong side of forty.)

Mr Cleaver has moved to Papua New Guinea. He wants to help the children over there by building a new school library and filling it with books donated from around the world. Apparently the school has no books and Mr Cleaver says it's a crying shame, so he's gone to do something about it. He is 'working for a cause', as Gran would say, which is an ADMIRABLE thing to do.

As for Miss Squirrel-Smith, she is lovely and not at all squirrel-like. She is tall and thin with long blonde hair and sky-blue eyes. She is very fit-looking, like an ironwoman or athlete.

Sporty. Pretty. Giggly. The perfect teacher for Portia.

But Miss Squirrel-Smith does DIGRESS a

lot. Like today when she was talking about geography, she digressed and started telling us about the time she backpacked through Istanbul, which is in Turkey, and nearly fell into the Bosphorus. My Gran told me once that the Bosphorus is like a huge harbour. She knows these things because she's a travel writer and goes to all these amazing places.

When Miss Squirrel-Smith was teaching

us geometry, she digressed again and started talking about the time she went hang-gliding and landed in a tree.

Miss Squirrel-Smith is so bright and bubbly that it's impossible not to like her or be swept away by her stories. But, as I said, she does digress a lot.

Before I digress any further – which is so totally easy to do when I have so many fun and exciting things to tell you – I need to backtrack slightly. To recap, so far this year I've been in a school musical, I've gone on a celebrity whirlwind ride with Portia when she wanted to be a famous model and I've been to Fiji with my Gran. Can you believe it? Are you jealous?

BTW, Gran is now on her way to Costa Rica so she can write her next travel book.

She rarely stays home.

The two weeks in Fiji was awesome. It was the best holiday ever and the first time we had been to Fiji. There was only one catch – we had to take our annoying seven-year-old next-door neighbour, Dillon Pickleton, with us.

Portia and I call him Dill Pickle. Teehee.

I did, however, start to like Dill a whole lot better while we were over there. Besides, I still had a fab time. How could you not in Fiji?

Right now, the next totally exciting thing I'm looking forward to is my birthday, which is only twenty-six sleeps away. I'm ten years old and very, very, very nearly eleven. It's so close I can almost touch it.

What could be better than being

eleven? I know I'm still way off teenage-hood, but at least eleven is one year closer. I'm sure when I do become a teenager, Mum will let me stay up much later than she does now. Fingers crossed, anyway.

Before I get into full swing with this new diary, I should tell you about my zany, whacky, out-there family. I must warn you, they are unusual. Especially Portia. If I explain their quirkiness now you might understand them better as they make special guest appearances throughout my diary. Portia is a good place to start. Most things usually start and end with her.

But you will have to wait a minute because Mum just got home and I want to say hello to her. Hang on.

Monday 3 May. 5:22 pm.

On the back porch, hanging in the hammock.

Okay, so I said hello to Mum and she's now locked in her art studio working on her latest masterpiece. Mum is using lots of white, baby-pink and lemon colours. It's all very pastel and very soft, which is nothing like Mum's usual creations. She sent me out of her studio though, so I couldn't get a good look at what she's painting. Maybe I will sneak in and have a look later. It might give me some clue as to why she's so preoccupied.

Now, where was I? Oh, yes, I remember: Portia.

# MY TWIN SISTER, PORTIA

Portia, being my identical twin, looks exactly, precisely like me. Except for a teardrop-shaped mole on my left cheek and maybe a few new freckles from Fiji, we look the same. But we are vastly different on the inside.

Portia is the total opposite of me. I'm shy and sensitive and very sensible. Mum's always telling me how sensible I am. Well, that might not be entirely true. I *wish* she would tell me how sensible I am, because I am sensible – and clever, and funny. But I digress ...

Portia, on the other hand, is confident and talented and outgoing. She is also capable of being rather bossy. She likes telling people what to do; although, she doesn't call it that. She says she's 'giving friendly advice' and 'mentoring'.

Sometimes her advice is helpful.

Other times, it is misguided and unhelpful.

Like the time Portia advised Jolie, our total BFF (best friend forever), about toilet training her kitten. As if Portia would know about kittens when she and Mum both refuse to let me have one. But that didn't stop Portia handing out her 'friendly advice'. She told Jolie she should teach her kitten, Jester, to use the human toilet. Poor Jester was so tiny and confused about the whole toilet issue that he fell into the bowl while Jolie was trying to teach him how to use it. Now the poor darling is so terrified of that big, white, nasty, wet thing that he won't go near any toilet. It's a good thing Jolie is happy with him being an outside cat. At least there are no toilets in her backyard to terrorise him.

Don't get me wrong, I love my sister to bits, but she does have her faults. I'm just pointing them out now so you know. I might point out her good points later. If I can think of any.

Portia is also messy, but I'm neat. Unfortunately for me, we share a room. Portia's side of the room is always a pigsty. Oink. Oink. Oink. I've had to draw a line down the middle of the room several times so Portia only messes her side and I can keep my side clean. Sometimes she just sweeps her toys and magazines and gadgets under the bed when Mum has told her to clean up. I'd never do that. Because Mum hasn't learned that she needs to check under the bed, Portia still gets her pocket money.

That is so not fair!

I've tried sending Mum SECRET SIGNALS to check under the bed before she hands over her cash, but Mum doesn't pick up on them. Either that, or Mum isn't game enough to stick her head under Portia's bed to see what's under there.

Come to think of it, I wouldn't be game either. I'm certain there are things decomposing under Portia's bed. That's why I keep air freshener handy. For someone so girly, Portia can be really grubby.

## MY MUM

My mum's name is Skye Emerald Pinchgut. She's fantastic and I totally love her. She's a yoga teacher, a laughter therapist and an artist. I kid you not.

Mum stretches herself a little thin sometimes – and I don't mean when she's doing her sun salutations in yoga. I mean that she struggles with juggling her work and being a single parent. I'd never tell her that though. She does try hard. She gives Portia and me quite a lot of freedom to do what we want, except when it comes to eating food like hot chips, lollies and chocolate. Mum's a vegetarian so she's super health conscious. She doesn't let much fast food into the house.

My parents are divorced. Mum has a nice boyfriend called Mr Divine. If I'm not mistaken, there may be some developments in the 'romance side' of things in their relationship, if you catch what I mean. Stay tuned.

## MY DAD

As for my dad, Pickford Rutherby Pinchgut (don't tell him I told you what his middle name is because he hates it), he lives in

21

England with his new wife. Dad tells me that he and his wife, Eleanor Elizabeth Krankston (or E.E.K. for short, which is what Portia and I call her), are in love. Blurh!

I don't need to know that stuff. I'm just glad Dad is happy. I miss him heaps, but he and Mum fought a lot when they were together so I know it's for the best that they now have new lives. Portia and I sometimes use Skype to call Dad, while other times we text or email him. Speaking of Skype, now that Mum has a new laptop (which Mr Divine bought for her while we were in Fiji) I think I will try to Skype Dad again soon.

Dad and EEK own a chocolate shop, which Mum, of course, doesn't approve of. Apparently EEK is also the heiress to a huge fortune. So Dad has done well for himself. Not that we see any of this newly acquired cash. The money isn't ours and I wouldn't feel comfortable taking any of it from Dad even if he did send it.

Portia has no such reservations. She said she would be happy to live like a princess if Dad wanted to fund her lifestyle. I, on the other hand, have scruples.

Gotta go. Mum is calling me to set the table for dinner.

TTFN (Ta Ta For Now).

# Thursday 6 May. 7:05 am.

In bed, having just woken up.

Portia is snoring her head off.

Extremely unattractive.

Twenty-three sleeps until my birthday. I've already made a list of presents I would like. I've taped it in below.

I don't think that's too much to ask the Birthday Fairy, do you?

BTW, I've wanted a kitten for ages. I think it has something to do with me liking everything Egyptian. Cats were super important to the Egyptians. In fact, the Egyptians loved and respected them so much they sometimes mummified them like they did the pharaohs.

# TOP TWELVE BIRTHDAY PRESENT WISH LIST

1. A kitten
2. iPad
3. Mobile phone
4. Hot air balloon ride
5. A kitten
6. A year's supply of purple gel pens (because they keep running out on me)
7. Antique Egyptian scarab pendant necklace (which I saw on eBay)
8. A kitten
9. A box of Velvet Chocolate fudge from the Fudge Kitchen
10. A new dress from Sadie's Funky Fashion Boutique
11. My own bedroom (because I'm tired of sharing with messy Portia)
12. A KITTEN, PLEASE

# Friday 7 May. 4:42 pm.

In my room. Twenty-two sleeps to go.

We are in a QUANDARY. Portia and I are facing a dilemma, a predicament, a fix, a jam, a sticky situation.

Why? Because we can't decide what theme to go with for our party. Or more accurately, we can't *agree* on the theme we want. This is the problem with having to share your birthday – and your party – with someone who is so totally different to you, and when your mum has a strict budget that she says can't be exceeded.

I'd like a PRINCESS PARTY. We could watch a movie, eat pizza and popcorn and have some pampering like a pedicure or something girlish. We could finish the night with a sleepover then have delicious pancakes in the morning. Doesn't that sound like awesome fun?

Mum likes this idea and thinks it will keep costs down. I thought Portia would like it too, seeing as how I built in girly aspects, which she loves.

But Portia said my PRINCESS PARTY was nowhere near good enough for an eleventh birthday party. She said it wasn't interesting or fun enough. She also insisted there was no way in the world she could limit herself to four guests like Mum said we had to. Instead, Portia wants a massive disco party with a DJ and disco ball and everything. She's so obsessed with dancing!

'This party is going to be a birthday bonanza,' she said. 'No, wait, make that a birthday extravaganza. It has to be the best party anyone at Heartfield Heights Primary School has ever had. We want everybody talking about it.'

'Why?' I asked her.

'Because we're trendsetters, sister dear, and trendsetters must always come up with the biggest and the best.'

This has left me with much to ponder.

# Friday 7 May. 5:27 pm.

Under the jacaranda tree, enjoying some peace and quiet.

Portia won't stop hassling me about this birthday party. I've heard enough about it today, but she is relentless. She showed me the incredibly long list of people she wants to invite. You should have seen it. There were about a hundred kids' names on it. People don't even have that many guests at weddings.

When I asked her about it, she wasn't very happy.

'Why do you want to invite Cleo Rasmussen?' I asked her. 'She was mean to you when you couldn't get Taylor North to come to her party.'

Taylor North is a famous actress who stars in *River's Town*, which is Portia's and my favourite TV show.

'Not couldn't, Perse, wouldn't,' Portia replied. 'I didn't want to invite Taylor North. Sure, Cleo was a smidgen selfish about the whole thing, but she's not so bad. She's a good person to have on our guest list. If other kids know she's coming they'll come to.'

I told Portia I would prefer not to go to a party Cleo was at, especially when it was my party. Portia sighed and crossed her name off.

Next on the list was Taylor North.

'Taylor North?' I said. 'She's never going to come to our lame suburban party. She's

a megastar and likes everyone to know it.'

Portia huffed and crossed Taylor North off too, claiming she didn't like her anyway and was only inviting her because she would add value to the party.

Next was a long list of sixth grade kids.

'Do they even know you exist?' I asked Portia. I thought this was a reasonable question, considering we are only in Year 5.

'Of course they do,' she insisted. 'I'm a celebrity, remember?'

Are you getting the picture that my sister has a big head? Or in other words, that she thinks very highly of herself – perhaps more highly than other people do?

'Maybe you were a celebrity for five seconds when you did some modelling,' I said, 'but that was weeks ago. People will have forgotten by now.'

Portia yelped like a puppy with a sore paw. 'I'm not forgotten,' she protested. 'My stint as a model helped my social rankings no end. And yours.'

'Whatever,' I said. 'They're not going to come to our party, okay?'

'All right, all right. I'll scrub them off too. There. Happy?'

'Ecstatic. At least I know most of the people on the list now.'

'Well, let's hope they talk to you,' Portia said, rather meanly.

Just then I began to wish something would happen to Portia that would put her in her place. And it did! Finally something went right for me and wrong for Portia. It was a MIRACLE.

While Portia was fuming and pouting and being rude, a pair of soaking wet, red-and-green striped undies flew over the fence and landed with a wet 'SMACK' right on top of Portia's head where they sat, dripping water (at least I hope it was water) down her face.

For several long seconds, Portia had this stunned look on her face like she'd woken up from a deep sleep and didn't know where she was.

I burst out laughing. Portia lifted the

soaking mass off her head and held it up, trying to identify what it was. When she realised they were undies she screamed and screamed and screamed.

I laughed so much I cried. My ribs ached.

Portia kept screaming.

Dill's head popped over the fence.

'Oh, hi, Perse-Portia!' he called. Dill often calls us 'Perse-Portia' or 'the twins' or some other joint name because he gets us mixed up. (BTW, he's not the only one.) 'Sorry, I think I kicked my undies over here when I was getting changed. Have you seen them?'

'Is this what you're looking for?' Portia growled, as she held the dripping wet undies aloft with a crooked finger.

Dill gulped. 'Um, yep, that's them.'

'Well, here!' Portia flung them back at him. 'They're all yours.' Then she turned and stormed into the house, taking her soggy guest list with her.

'Did you do that intentionally?' I asked, wiping my eyes and trying to stifle a new eruption of laughter.

'No,' Dill said. 'I was getting out of the pool and kicked them too high when I was getting changed.'

'You've got a pool?' I asked excitedly. 'Since when?' I was considering the possibility of going next door for a swim. The weather had been all over the place and it was actually quite warm for May.

Dill's face turned as red as the stripes on his undies. 'Um, it's a paddling pool. You can come over and use it whenever you want.'

I was completely disappointed now. No way was I interested in a baby pool so I told him, 'No thanks.'

'If you ever change your mind, you know where I live.'

Then we stood there for a while until Dill eventually asked, 'Is a penguin a bird or a fish? I can never work it out.'

I laughed. Dill turned scarlet.

mean a fish,' he floundered.

it lives in the water and on the land. It has to be an anphibian, like one of those Mexican walking fish, doesn't it?'

'Am-phibian. Not an-phibian.'

'So is it one?'

'One what?'

'I don't know: bird, fish, amphibian? What is it?'

'It's a bird, Dill,' I said. 'A penguin is a bird.'

'Oh. Thanks, Perse-Portia.'

Then Dill ran off, leaving me to the twin quandaries of penguins and parties.

Just so you know, Mum will never allow Portia to invite everyone on her list; and Portia will never accept no for an answer.

This could get interesting.

Determined to sort out the matter of our impending birthday party, Portia dragged me into Mum's studio so we could discuss it with her. But when we got there, Mum wasn't painting. She was in the middle of a secret telephone conversation. Which is why she was hiding in the studio.

'We need to talk to you about something important,' Portia said.

Mum covered the mouthpiece. 'I'm on the phone, girls.'

Portia asked who to and Mum blushed and said, 'It's Will. Now, do you mind? Off you go.' Will is Mr Divine, Mum's

41

boyfriend.

'I don't mind,' Portia said, all innocent. She folded her arms and looked at Mum, waiting for her to hang up.

Mum waved at Portia and me and said, 'Nice try. Now, out you go. I'll talk to you in a minute.'

Sigh. Still no answer to our problems.

Monday 10 May. 8:15 pm.
In my room.

Portia and I are holed up in our room while Mum teaches her Monday night yoga class. We just finished designing our party invitations so now I'm writing this – pretending to do my homework – while Portia reads a fashion magazine. Even though we still don't have a theme for the party, Portia said we should at least design something and get it ready. It helped pass the time too.

We designed the invitations on Mum's laptop. I'm really pleased with how they look. I've printed one off and stuck it in here for you. I think it's great how we

Persephone
and Portia's
11th Birthday
Party

For: _____
Date: _____
Time: _____
Place: _____
R.S.V.P.: _____

both got to put pink and purple on there, our two favourite colours.

Hey, I know, I'll Skype Dad later to ask his advice about the party. I'll fill you in on what he says.

# Tuesday 11 May. 7:45 am.

In the kitchen, eating breakfast.

Eighteen sleeps to go.

I Skyped Dad last night. It was so great talking to him! I forgot how much I miss him. He was quite chatty, asking me about school and Fiji. He even mentioned our birthday. I wonder what he'll send us this year. I hope it's not money again.

Don't get me wrong, money does come in handy, but as a present from your dad it's kind of lame. It shows he's out of touch or doesn't know you so well. I'd like him to send me something English, something special I can't get over here. I guess we'll have to wait and see.

Unfortunately, you can't send kittens in the post.

Portia, as usual, butted in on my conversation to Dad. She has a habit of taking over things. At least she asked good questions though. She put Dad on the spot, actually.

When she asked him how the chocolate shop was doing and if he was rich yet, he said, 'Well, Portia, these things take time, you know.'

Then she asked him where EEK was. Only she didn't say 'EEK' because that would be rude. She said very politely, 'Where is Eleanor, Dad?'

Usually when we Skype or phone Dad you can hear – and sometimes see – EEK in the background. She always puts her two cents into the conversation even when we don't want her to. Sometimes it's nice just having a private conversation with Dad, which EEK doesn't always understand.

Last night, however, EEK was nowhere to be seen.

Dad said she was lying down. He had this weird look on his face like he wasn't telling us the full story.

'Is she sick?' Portia asked. 'It's the middle of the day over there, isn't it?'

Dad said, 'Not quite. She's not sick, just resting.'

Portia shot me a SECRET SIGNAL of disapproval, which I hope Dad didn't see.

I have to agree with Portia. Perhaps if you're born into wealth and privilege like EEK was it's totally okay to lie down in the middle of the day and have your servants do things. However, you would never catch my hard-working mum doing such a thing. But I digress, I guess.

Then Portia noticed a stack of cardboard boxes behind Dad. She's good with things like that. 'Are those boxes of chocolate behind you, Dad?' she asked.

Dad gave a strangled cough and said they weren't boxes of chocolate, just boxes. After that, he said he had to go and he hung up.

Portia and I thought it was strange to have so many messy boxes sitting in a room. We discussed the matter for some time after the video call, but couldn't work out why he would have them so we went to sleep none the wiser.

This morning it occurred to me that Dad might have gone into another type of business where he had to buy lots of stuff to sell. Maybe the boxes were part of that. When I mentioned it to Portia she pointed out that Dad would have said so if that was the case. I told her that maybe he didn't want us getting excited about his new business.

Portia snorted. 'I doubt it. I think the clues are pointing to the fact that he and EEK are splitting up and Dad is moving out of their apartment.' She shrugged. 'It looks pretty obvious to me: no EEK and plenty of boxes. They've split up for sure.'

Portia seemed so certain that now I'm beginning to worry. I know I say rude things about EEK, but I don't want her and Dad to split up. I want Dad to be happy. I don't want him to be sad and lonely in England. I couldn't bear that.

Wednesday 12 May. 7:22 pm.

On the back porch.

We finally managed to pin Mum down and ask her about the birthday party details. She said a definite no to a DISCO PARTY because it would cost too much and annoy the neighbours, but agreed a PRINCESS PARTY and sleepover would be perfect. Portia pouted about this decision for a full twenty minutes.

I was elated because, as you can probably guess, I rarely get my way around here.

 So a PRINCESS PARTY it is! It's going to be awesome. Portia printed the invitations. I'm not

sure what took her so long, but she finally finished. We filled them out together so we can hand them out tomorrow.

While Portia was inside printing the invitations, I stayed back with Mum. She was weeding her herb garden. It's rare that I get one-on-one time with Mum, so I took the opportunity while I could.

I also wanted to talk to her about Dad. I told her about the boxes I'd seen at his place and asked whether she thought Dad and Eleanor were splitting up.

Mum stopped weeding. She plucked a stem of coriander and chewed on it. She handed me a stem too and said it helped relieve anxiety. I started chewing and asked her again about Dad and Eleanor. She told me the last she'd heard they were happy and in love.

'What if that's changed?' I asked.

Mum assured me that Dad would work through it, and that he was a 'big boy' and could take care of himself.

I asked her if she still cared about him.

Mum stopped chewing and looked at me for a while. Her eyes went kind of red and I could tell she was sad. She told me she would always care about him because he was the father of her two beautiful daughters (emphasis here on BEAUTIFUL), but that she had moved on.

'I'm sure if Pickton needs anything, he'll let us know.' Mum handed me another coriander stem. She told me not to worry or read too much into things, and that Dad and Eleanor were perfectly fine.

I nodded again, mainly because I couldn't talk at that moment because a huge, hot lump was sitting in my throat and I knew if I tried to talk I'd cry.

Mum smiled and hugged me and said that we were perfectly fine too. 'My work is going well,' she said. 'You and your sister are doing great at school. You have a birthday party coming up. Life is good, Perse. So you, my darling, don't need to worry so much.'

She picked up her basket of fresh coriander, parsley, tomatoes and carrots and said we would have salad for dinner because the tasty organic food would make us feel better.

We went inside. I helped Mum make the salad and her awesome mustard and vinegar dressing. Mum was right. The salad did make me feel better.

Until Mum dropped her BOMBSHELL.

Gotta go. Portia is finally out of the shower and it's my turn now. I hope she's left me some hot water. Back soon.

# Wednesday 12 May. 9:07 pm.

One last entry before I go to sleep.

Sorry to do that to you, but when the bathroom becomes free in this place you have to make the most of it.

Okay, so where was I? Oh, yes. Mum's bombshell.

Are you ready for it?

Are you sitting down?

I nearly fainted when I heard this, so I want to make sure you're prepared.

All right, here goes. Deep breath.

Mum and Mr Divine are getting engaged.

Yes, you heard it correctly.

Engaged.

Engaged to be married.

EEEEKKKKKK!

# Thursday 13 May. 7:51 am.

Sitting at my desk.

The atmosphere in the house is not very nice this morning. Portia is still giving Mum the silent treatment after last night's announcement.

Portia was thumping around our room getting dressed and muttering under her breath about life being 'so unfair' and about certain 'selfish' people we live with. I told her to get a grip and that we should be happy for Mum. Portia's head nearly blew off at that. She said I obviously had no idea what Mum's engagement would do to our lives. She also made a comment about me being her 'naive little sister'.

Portia likes to call me her little sister to put me in my place because she is a whole, entire two minutes older than me.

'We might have to move house,' she continued. 'We might have to change schools. We might lose our friends. Do you get the picture now?'

Once again, I was left with much to ponder.

# Thursday 13 May. 6:47 pm.

In the lounge room, waiting for *River's Town* to come on. Sixteen sleeps to go.

Mission accomplished! Portia and I finally handed out our birthday invitations, so it's official: we're having a party, a celebration, a gathering, a shindig, a bash.

Admittedly, it didn't take us long to hand out the invitations. We're only inviting four people. But at least they're super cool.

Here's the run-down on our guests-to-be.

## Jolie Anderson

My total BFF since kindergarten. She's smart, funny, sensitive and caring. A lot like me, really. Often when I'm upset with Portia I'll tell Jolie about it. She's excellent at finding solutions to problems.

## Caitlin Marciano

My other total BFF since kindergarten. Along with Jolie and Portia, we're a solid gang of four who do everything together. Caitlin is loads of fun even though she's giggly like Portia. They do ballet together. Caitlin is Italian. She has to put up with three brothers. Yikes! Can you imagine?

# Hayley Carrington

Hayley is an awesome flute player and one of the girls in our class. Hayley loves animals almost as much as I do, so I think she is pretty cool, even if she does try too hard to get Portia's attention.

# Charlotte Briar

Charlotte is Hayley's BFF. They've known each other since they were babies and their mums were in mother's group together. They're almost as inseparable as Portia and me, although Miss Squirrel-Smith said the other day she would have to split Hayley and Charlotte up if they didn't stop talking.

Charlotte is very good at talking. She's also excellent at maths and science. I wish I was as smart as her.

Anyway, Portia and I handed the invitations out first thing in the morning and then spent the rest of the day (whenever we weren't in class, that is) planning the party. We talked about the food we would have, what clothes we would wear, how we would do our hair, what movies we would watch and that sort of thing.

I started making a list of everything we needed.

So we wouldn't forget.

And because I like lists.

# Here is a list of the party food we will need:

1. Popcorn
2. Salt and vinegar crisps
3. Creaming soda (sugar-free, of course)
4. Chocolate (assuming Mum lets chocolate into the house for our birthday)
5. Marshmallows
6. Vegetarian rolls (because Mum won't let us eat meaty sausage rolls, I'm sure)
7. Mini pizzas
8. Vanilla Oreos
9. Ice-cream
10. Cake! Cake! Cake!

There was one problem at lunchtime. Portia disappeared. I couldn't find her anywhere, which is odd because Portia and I always hang out together. Also, because we have the party to plan you'd think we'd be hanging out more than ever.

When I quizzed her about her mysterious disappearance, she brushed me off. Hmmm, curious. Maybe she's worried about Mum's impending engagement. Maybe she wanted private time to think about it. I don't know, and she won't tell me.

She did seem to have loads of pink and purple ink on her hands though. I wonder what that's all about. If you ask me, everyone is acting strange lately. First Mum (although now I know why) then

Dad (still to get to the bottom of that one) and now Portia (admittedly, she does act strange on a regular basis).

Am I the only normal one in my family?

Wait. Don't answer that. I already know I am.

Saturday 15 May. 9:07 am.

In the bathroom trying to write a

private diary entry.

While Portia was getting extra beauty sleep this morning – snoring her head off while the day got into full swing – Mum dropped BOMBSHELL NUMBER TWO. She thought she would try the idea on me first before presenting it to Portia. Divide and conquer, I guess. She knows I'm okay with the whole Mr Divine thing. Portia is 'another matter altogether', as Gran would say.

At the moment, except for when she is talking about our party, Portia's rather stroppy and short with everyone. She's definitely not coping with things.

Mum's bombshell isn't going to help. She wants us to ... wait for it ... meet Mr Divine's parents! She says we're becoming one big family so we need to get to know each other.

I asked Mum when she planned on telling Portia about this latest development. She said she was waiting for the right time. I told her that there probably wasn't ever going to be a right time, and that she should tell Portia right away. Mum seemed nervous about doing that. She said she didn't want to upset Portia any more than she had to.

I asked, 'When are we meeting them?'

'Tomorrow,' Mum said.

While I was considering the implications

of this, Mum added, 'And you have to stop calling him Mr Divine, Perse. You can call him Will. He'll eventually be your stepdad, you know. You can't call him Mr Divine then.'

'I'm not sure I'm ready to call him Will,' I said. I wasn't sure I was ready for him to be my stepdad either, but I didn't say this. I don't like the word 'stepdad'.

As if echoing my thoughts, Portia shouted, 'He'll never be my stepdad, so you can forget about that.'

Mum and I looked over and saw her standing in the doorway, still wearing her pyjamas and with her hair messy from bed. After that, Portia stormed around the house making loud noises before locking herself in our bedroom, where she's been

ever since. She turned her music up super loud and wouldn't answer the door to Mum.

Now Mum is knocking on the bathroom door where I am. She asked me to convince Portia to come out of her room and deal with this engagement thing. So, it's up to me to sort Portia out. I don't know how much luck I'll have. I yelled out to Mum that I was coming, so I'd better go. I will update you soon.

PS Not much to celebrate at the moment, but fourteen sleeps to go.

In the lounge room.

I finally managed to get Portia out of her room, although she's still sulky. She's taking this Mr Divine thing – I mean the Will thing – hard.

'Aren't you happy the way things are with Mum and you and me living together? Just the three of us?' Portia asked me.

I told her I was, but reminded her that Mum really likes Mr Divine. I also admitted it might be useful and fun having a man around the house again.

Portia, as I mentioned before, always acts so strong and confident and certain. But right then she started crying and said she was afraid that having Mr Divine around would change everything, including Mum.

'We've just gotten used to Dad leaving and now someone new comes along. This means more change. Speaking of Dad, I'm worried about him. I miss him SO MUCH, Perse. I secretly always hoped that he and Mum would get back together, that he might leave EEK and come home and everything would be good again. I hoped there would be this happy ending like in fairytales and we could be a family again.'

I hugged her then and let her cry for a while.

Sometimes it's best to let it out.

I never knew Portia felt this way. Deep down it's what I've always wanted too. I admitted this to her and then said, 'But it's not going to happen. That dream we have, that wish that Mum and Dad get back together, is just that. It's a wish. Life isn't like that. Remember how much Mum and Dad used to fight when they were together? They were sad all the time. Now they're happy. They're much better off following their own paths. We're better off too.'

Portia wiped her eyes and nodded and said she supposed I was right. I suggested we get to know Mr Divine better and see what happens. I also reminded her that no matter what we'd always have each other.

'Perse,' Portia sniffed, 'sometimes you're so clever and sensible and reliable. I know I don't say it much, but you're the best sister ever.' Then she made me promise I'd never leave her.

This made my day – or maybe even my year – because Portia rarely says mushy things like that. I promised, and hugged her again. I told her we'd try to Skype Dad again, and that she shouldn't worry so much because Dad was probably fine and we were fine too. Just like Mum told me before.

Portia was happy with that and she's now gone to ballet class with Caitlin. I'm hanging at home, writing in my diary and reading my Egyptian archaeology book.

Portia apologised to Mum before she left. They had a big hug, too, and Mum told us both that everything would be all right.

Mum is going out to dinner with Mr Divine tonight. Mrs Pickleton from next door is minding us. Portia had to bite her tongue on that one because she hates being babysat, but she is obviously trying to go easy on Mum. For now.

# Saturday 15 May. 9:45 pm.

Tucked up in bed.

YAWN! I'm just about to turn off the light after a huge emotional rollercoaster of a day. It's taxing having a sister like Portia.

We tried Skyping Dad but he wasn't online. Mrs Pickleton came over to mind us and she brought Dill with her because her husband was on duty. He's a fireman.

Nee-nah. Nee-nah.

Portia is still grumbling about the wet undies incident. I wish I had that on video!

Dill is trying to win Portia over big time. He can't stand her being angry with him. 'Perse-Portia,' he said, 'I have a joke for you.'

**Portia** (in a grouchy tone): 'What is it?'

**Dillon**: 'What did one tree say to the other tree?'

**Portia**: 'I have no idea.'

**Dillon**: 'Hey, we're trees!'

**Portia**: Unprintable comment mumbled before storming off.

**Dillon**: 'I guess she didn't like my joke.'

**Me:** 'It's not you, Dill. It's her.'

**Dillon**: 'Yeah, thought so. Hey, do you want to play a game?'

At least he's the kind of kid who bounces back easily.

As a special treat, Mrs Pickleton brought over ice-cream that she'd made in her new ice-cream maker. She served up the blueberry and cookies ice-cream in waffle cones. Delicious! As Dill carried

Portia's ice-cream to her, I saw him lick it a few times before he handed it over (it was kind of soft and melty).

Portia didn't notice because she was reading her magazine. I didn't say anything, although I did have a quiet giggle to myself.

Dill sat down. 'I love you,' he said to his ice-cream before devouring it.

This made me giggle some more. Portia rolled her eyes and kept eating her pre-licked ice-cream, which made me giggle even more.

When I told Dill he was a funny kid, he replied, 'I'm not a kid. I'm seven years old.'

Sometimes he cracks me up.

I played Monopoly with Dill to pass the

time. Poor Dill got so tired he fell asleep at the table. When Mum came home she showed us the engagement ring Will gave her at dinner. It's a pink diamond. Super beautiful and shiny! Portia, of course, now wants a pink diamond of her own.

Mrs Pickleton had to wake Dill up to take him home. He got cranky and said he wanted to go back to sleep because he was watching a dream.

Oh, I forgot to mention that we're off to meet Mr Divine's parents tomorrow. I hope we like them. I hope they like us. Pretty soon we'll be one big family.

I hope it's a happy family.

# Sunday 16 May. 9:20 pm.

I'm in bed again. (I have been out, I promise!) Thirteen sleeps to go, but who's counting?

Phew! What a day. I don't think I've ever eaten so much in my life, except in Fiji where we had those all-you-can-eat buffets for breakfast, lunch and dinner.

Let me start by saying that Mr Divine's house wasn't what I was expecting.

Not in a million years.

Not only is it technically not his house (he lives with his parents even though he's getting on in years and is well over thirty), but his house – or the house – is MASSIVE.

It's this huge, rambling, white brick MANSION with gigantic windows from one end to the other that have leadlight coloured glass in them. It has two storeys and a black tiled roof with chimneys sprouting everywhere. It even has turrets and round rooms with pointy rooves on top like castles. All it needs is a few knights in shining armour.

It has gardens with huge lawns and trees and bushes snipped into shapes. It has a high metal fence all the way round with automatic gates and a gravel driveway leading through a forest on the way to the house. It also has fountains and statues everywhere.

It is basically a PALACE.

You should have seen Portia's eyes light up when she saw it. For the first time in days she stopped pouting, and then started fidgeting with her hair and her dress and peeking in the car's rear-view mirror. When I asked her what was up, she said, 'Nothing. Just making sure I look my best for our new relatives.'

I should have known. The palace has turned Portia's head and changed her opinion of Mr Divine.

Portia squeezed my hand. 'Imagine having our party here, Perse. Wouldn't it be fabulous?'

I whispered, 'No, because it's not our house and you haven't even met Mr Divine's parents yet. They could be total ogres.'

Portia giggled and told me not to be silly. She was certain the Divines would be as divine as their house. Then she asked Mum and Mr Divine (who was driving) whether we would be moving here after the wedding.

Yes, now she wants to move!

Thankfully, Mum said no, that we would be staying right where we were and that Mr Divine didn't want to live here anymore because he wanted to move in with us and do some renovations and help Mum pay the mortgage.

Always looking for an opportunity, Portia asked whether we could put on an extra storey so she could have her own room.

Mum said, 'That's a long way down the track, Portia. Can we please just get today out of the way? Now, girls, best behaviour.'

I noticed Mum chewing her fingernails. I asked her what was wrong, knowing straight away that she was nervous. She laughed and looked sideways at Mr Divine. I mean Will. Mum said she hoped she would make a good impression.

I patted her shoulder from the backseat and reassured her. Will agreed.

'What about Perse and me?' Portia

asked. 'Do you think they'll like us?'

Mum smiled and said they might if we behaved ourselves and didn't bicker.

Ha-ha, I thought, very funny.

We pulled up on the circular driveway beside the fountain. Portia's eyes glinted. She burst out of the car and bolted up the white marble steps to greet her 'new relatives', as she insisted on calling them.

Luckily for her (and Mum), Mr Divine's

parents were super nice. Apparently, Mr Divine's mum, Alice, is a famous sculptor. His dad, Trevor, is a banker. They're both retired now, but that's how they made their money. BTW, they have a housekeeper and a gardener.

Mr Divine seems to have inherited his mother's artistic talent. Several of his paintings were hanging up in the halls. He didn't tell me this, his mum did. She is clearly super proud of her son.

They showed us around the entire 'estate' and put up with Portia's endless questions and my shyness. They served delicious food and even had those chocolate coins wrapped in gold foil as a treat for Portia and me. It was probably a bit babyish, but I didn't mind because I love chocolate. Mum didn't even protest about the high level of caffeine and sugar in it either, which she usually does. I guess Mum was on her best behaviour too.

So the day went fantastically, smashingly, wonderfully well. We all came home happy and content, especially Mum.

## Monday 17 May. 8:04 am.

Eating honey toast on the back porch.

Twelve sleeps to go.

I'm having a quiet moment to myself before the onslaught of school. I think I have a bad case of Monday-itis. I wish it was still the weekend!

I can't stop thinking about yesterday at Mr Divine's house. I saved one of those foil-wrapped chocolate coins. It's in my uniform pocket now. I seriously considered scoffing it for breakfast, but have decided to keep it for morning tea instead. Let's see if it survives. Besides, I want to show Jolie and Caitlin the chocolate coin so they believe me when I tell them about Mr Divine's palace.

Portia is almost back to normal this morning. From what I've seen of her, that is. She's currently locked in the bathroom brushing her hair and getting ready for school. Typical Portia, she's taking about four hours to get ready. I have to sign off now so I can drag her out and make sure we're not late. She said she had something to talk to me about on the way to school. I'm dying to find out what it is. I'll fill you in as soon as I know.

TTFN.

# Tuesday 18 May. 4:51 pm.

In the hammock.

You are never going to guess what crazy plan Portia has come up with now. This is one of her best-ever schemes. She may just be clever enough to pull it off.

Yesterday, she strung me out all through school, refusing to tell me what she had planned. She said she was going to tell me but then decided it would be better to show me.

It was only when we were walking home from school that Portia came clean. We were passing the shopping centre, where I'd noticed this new cake shop that had opened a few weeks ago. I wasn't the only one. Nearly every kid at school had noticed. Portia and I had discussed it more than once. We know Mum won't ever let us go into the shop because she believes sugar is the worst thing you can eat.

This shop is so gorgeous, with its window displays of real cakes and the heavenly sweet, sugary, chocolaty aromas floating out to torment and tempt you.

When I asked who, she answered, 'Mr Divine.'

'No!' I said. 'Portia, you can't.'

'Can't what?'

'Can't whatever you're going to do. You know, manipulate poor Mr Divine.'

Portia laughed. She denied having any intention of manipulating anyone.

'However,' she held up her finger, 'there is cake to be had here, Perse, and I'm going to get it if it's the last thing I do. If Mr Divine wants to be part of our family, he needs to understand what makes us tick. He needs to make us happy and do things that we like, like buying us cake.'

I shook my head. I've seen Portia come up with some crazy plans before, but this takes the cake: literally.

When I told her that she couldn't make Mr Divine pay for the cake, not in a million years, she smiled and said. 'Oh, yes I can. Just watch me.'

PS We're not obsessed by cake, really we're not.

# Wednesday 19 May. 6:42 pm.

On my bed.

Monday's conversation with Portia (and the memory of that amazing cake) keeps whirling around in my head. I have no idea how she's going to make that cake happen for our party, but if I know Portia she'll give it a good go. The opportunity may come this weekend.

It seems Portia isn't the only one wanting people to know what makes her 'tick'. Will wants us to know what makes him tick too. Starting with camping.

The last time we went camping was about four years ago. It rained the entire time. Portia and I pretty much got pneumonia. Mum hated every minute of it and said she would never set foot inside a tent again. Not unless the sky turned green.

Well, the sky hasn't turned green, but Mum is going camping again. She wants to please Will and says we all have to go.

Portia hasn't stopped moaning about it. She pointed out that we didn't have any camping equipment because we sold it all after the last outdoor disaster.

Mum countered with, 'Will has plenty of camping equipment, Portia.'

Portia tried her 'wild animal' card, claiming they were dangerous and vicious.

I couldn't let this one slip. I'm not big on camping, but I won't have Portia denigrating our cute and cuddly native animals. 'You mean possums? Koalas? You think they're going to hurt you?' I said.

Portia insisted that male kangaroos could rip your insides out and that rats spread disease.

'Rats?' I said. 'In the bush?'

'Yes, rats, and bats and owls and foxes. They're deadly.'

I argued that no animals were as dangerous or destructive as humans and that most animals were afraid of us and would run away if we went near them.

Mum shouted at us to stop arguing and said we were going camping no matter what. Then she ordered us to pack up the dinner plates and tidy the kitchen because her yoga class was starting and she needed to get in the right frame of mind for it.

End of conversation.

PS Ten sleeps to go.

# Wednesday 19 May. 8:07 pm.

Still on my bed.

Mum's yoga almost over.

Portia is fuming about this camping trip. It's impossible living with someone who has such extremities of behaviour.

Speaking of extremities, I'd better make sure I pack plenty of warm clothes for the weekend so I don't lose *my* extremities. The weather is getting chilly now.

I made a list of all the important things we need to take with us when we go camping.

P.T.O. (Please Turn Over).

# Top Ten things I want to take on the camping trip

1. Hot water bottle

2. Shower (teehee, I know that one isn't going to happen)

3. Flushing toilet (alas, neither will that one)

4. A very warm and woolly jumper

5. Books

6. Hiking boots

7. Bandaids

8. Salt (to take care of leeches)

9. Hot chocolate (to warm me up at night)

10. This diary (to record the brilliant adventures we'll have. Not.)

Portia tried reading over my shoulder. She said I should add insect repellent to my list so that we have protection from mosquitoes and don't get malaria.

I told her she should pay more attention in class.

Uh-oh. The doorbell just rang. That is a big no-no when Mum is running her yoga class. She even has a sign taped up that says:

QUIET PLEASE!
YOGA CLASS IN PROGRESS
DO NOT RING DOORBELL
UNDER ANY CIRCUMSTANCES

I wonder who would be game enough to ring the doorbell when it has that sign plastered to it. This had better be good.

# Wednesday 19 May. 8:34 pm.

In my room, quickly scribbling in my diary.

I hope you are sitting down. Pandemonium has broken loose!

You will never guess who rang the doorbell.

Can't write now.

Far too much happening!

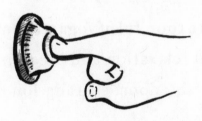

# Thursday 20 May. 4:02 pm.

At my desk.

Wow, the house is so packed. Mum let Portia and me skip school today. We were far too excited to go to anyway and Mum said one day off wouldn't hurt.

One day off to do what, you ask?

Before I tell you, I have to rewind a fraction.

Let's go back to last night when the doorbell rang.

Mum still had a roomful of yoga students doing their final relaxation and breathing exercises when the doorbell rang loudly and insistently.

Portia and I snuck out of our room. Mum was sitting in the lotus position giving the door a dirty look. The bell kept ringing.

I whispered to Mum, asking whether I should open the door. Mum nodded and apologised to her students, saying it must be urgent.

They were stretching and standing up as Portia and I weaved our way to the door. When we got there and opened the door who should we see standing on our front porch but ... Dad!!!! That's right, it was none other than Pickford Pinchgut, who we thought was in England.

Portia and I gave twin squeals and jumped into Dad's arms, hugging and kissing him. It was the best-ever reunion. He looked thinner and greyer than when we last saw him in person. Skype didn't show that up. He was happy to see us and we were trying to bring him inside, but there were all these yoga people in the way. Mum was saying goodbye to them all and at the same time asking, 'Who is it, girls?'

We couldn't answer because we were firing a million questions at Dad, asking him what he was doing here and when he'd gotten in and how long he'd be staying for.

Dad wasn't getting much of a word in and the yoga people were still streaming out of the house. Finally they left and it calmed down for a second, until Portia spotted someone standing in the shadows outside.

'Who's that?' she asked suspiciously.

Dad said he had someone for us to meet. He stepped back and revealed a woman who I hadn't noticed in the kerfuffle.

I blinked under the moth-filled porch light. Eleanor Elizabeth Krankston was standing there in the flesh! She looked totally tiny and pitifully pale, like she hadn't caught a decent splash of sunshine all her life. I guess she hasn't because I hear they don't get much sun in England.

I say she was tiny.

She was.

Except for one thing.

Which was totally huge.

Now, I've seen Mum make this mistake before with Mrs Atherton two doors down. Mrs Atherton has twelve kids. She's what Gran calls, a 'natural mother'. Once, when Mum thought Mrs Atherton was having another baby, she commented that she was 'glowing' and that pregnancy was agreeing with her and asked how far along she was. Mrs Atherton burst into tears and said she wasn't any way along and the only reason she looked like she was expecting was because her body hadn't bounced back after the last time.

Since then, even when Mrs Atherton did become pregnant again, Mum refused to mention it. According to Mum, there is no greater shame than asking a non-pregnant woman how pregnant she is.

So, when I saw EEK and noticed that the rather large part of her was out the front (imagine if it was out the back!) and I suspected she might be having a baby, I still couldn't bring myself to say anything.

Besides which, I was in total shock at the very thought of it because:

a) Dad had never mentioned anything.

b) It would mean I was about to get another brother or sister.

c) I had no idea how I felt about the whole thing.

None of that mattered because Portia also noticed EEK's bump. Her eyes went huge and round and she screamed, 'Dad, are you having a baby?'

At that precise moment, Mum appeared on the front porch looking beautiful and trim in her yoga tights and asked, 'What's all the fuss about?'

She saw Dad, and then EEK, and then looked from one to the other for what seemed the longest time, without saying anything.

I was sending her SECRET SIGNAL after SECRET SIGNAL, begging her to say something. Anything. Unfortunately, Mum is nowhere near as good as Portia at picking up my SECRET SIGNALS so she missed them (or ignored them).

We all stood there staring at each other until EEK gave a whispery sigh and fainted. It's lucky Dad was there to catch her because otherwise she might have hit her head.

'Have you got any more surprises for us?' Mum asked Dad, as we carried EEK inside and laid her down on the couch.

Dad coughed and asked whether there might be a spare room for him and EEK to stay in.

Mum thought he was joking, but no, he was super serious. He said he was broke, skint, completely out of cash. He said he'd barely had enough money to make it home and that the chocolate shop had gone under.

'Under what?' Portia asked.

Mum and I both shushed Portia at this.

EEK started waking up, although she still looked super pale and ill.

'Are you feeling all right, dear?' Mum shouted, as though EEK was deaf. Mum used a superior tone, like she was so much more elegant and refined than EEK, when we all know EEK comes from a prim and posh family.

Hang on. Someone is knocking at my bedroom door.

# Thursday 20 May. 6:18 pm.
At my desk. Again.

Sorry, I got called into a family meeting. There is loads to discuss since Dad and EEK moved in. But I digress.

I still have to fill you in about last night's SURPRISE ARRIVAL.

Portia was a mess, asking questions and giving EEK plenty of NOT-SO-SECRET SIGNALS that said, 'Please go home!'

Dad asked Mum to hear him out. She sat at the table and listened to the sad story of the FAILURE OF HIS BUSINESS and the loss of EEK's fortune, which led them here.

It seems, EEK's so-called fortune

wasn't as large as Portia had dreamed it to be. Now Dad and EEK have no money and nowhere to live, so Mum graciously moved her paintings to one side of her studio and they're staying in there.

Dad has promised he will be back on his feet soon. He bought the newspaper today and has lined up some job interviews, but he says the job market is slow at the moment and he doesn't know how good his 'prospects' are. Whatever a 'prospect' is.

Portia is trying her last ditch effort to get Mum and Dad back together. She keeps bringing out the photo albums and forcing Dad to look at them. She also keeps bringing up all the things we used to do together.

This morning she said, 'Hey, remember the time we went to the Easter Fair and Perse got lost and the police had to be called in to find her?'

Dad frowned. 'I'd rather forget about that.'

Me too, I thought.

Then she said, 'Weren't Perse and I adorable when we were babies, Dad?'

'Yes, until you learned to talk,' Dad joked.

Dad has helped around the house though. He fixed the toilet cistern, which has been leaking for three months and driving me crazy with its constant 'whish-whish-whish' noise. He also fixed a floorboard on the front porch that EVERYONE trips over.

Mum told Dad he didn't need to do so much around the house and that Will helped her with that stuff now.

Dad said he was only trying to be useful, and quick as a flash Mum came back with, 'Bit late for that, isn't it?'

I'm sure she didn't mean to be mean, it just came out wrong. Either way, Dad's shoulders drooped and he shuffled away to hide in the studio.

# Thursday 20 May. 10:41 pm.

Tucked up in bed, writing by torchlight.

I'm not the only one who can't sleep. Portia has had me up half the night, nattering about Dad and Mum and EEK and Mr Divine. I mean Will. She is over the moon that Dad has returned, but remains unimpressed with EEK. She has made that glaringly obvious to everyone.

Portia spent most of tonight making rude comments to EEK. I think she may be cross about the soon-to-be baby.

BTW, I must stop calling her EEK. I almost slipped up and called her EEK to her face at dinner.

Eleanor. Eleanor. Eleanor.

All these name changes are impossible to get used to!

I asked Mum what Mr Divine thought about Dad and Eleanor being here, and Mum said she had phoned him and that he had been very understanding.

I hope that's true.

I'm super curious about Eleanor and the baby-to-be. We actually had some time alone this afternoon. Ever since she got here she has been very quiet. I think she's missing home and finding it difficult being in Mum's house. It probably is an unusual situation, but that's my family for you.

When Eleanor and I were alone together, she told me all about her childhood. She explained how she lived on a huge property in the country in a large 'historic house' and rode horses and did showjumping and that sort of thing. She said she could drive a tractor by the age of eight. Can you believe it?

I asked her when the baby was due and she said not for a few months. She

said she hadn't been to regular doctors' appointments back in England because she and Dad hadn't been able to afford it.

I tell you, she is huge.

# Friday 21 May. 7:04 am.

At the breakfast table.

Yawn! I hardly got any sleep worrying about Dad and Eleanor last night. I really don't want to go to school.

# Friday 21 May. 7:48 am.

Sitting next to my bed.

Whenever Portia is upset or moody or angry or worried or ... anything ... she takes it out on me. A few minutes ago we were in the bathroom and she pushed her head next to mine and insisted we count our freckles in the mirror.

'Now we're getting older,' she said, 'I want to see if we start looking different.'

'We're identical, Portia,' I reminded her. 'We look the same.'

'To the untrained eye we look the same,' Portia replied. 'But you and I both know there are minute differences about our appearance that will probably get bigger

127

as we get older.'

'So?'

'So, I want to see which one of us gets the good changes.'

I told her she was impossible and she giggled, called me silly and told me to stay still so she could count my freckles.

In case you haven't realised, Portia does not like freckles. I knew what she was doing. She was trying to point out that I had more freckles than her so she could make herself feel better. Typical Portia. Lucky that sort of thing doesn't worry me. I think freckles add character to a face. And I told her so.

Portia gave up on the freckle issue and instead started on my nose. 'You know, I think your nose is a smidgen bigger than

mine,' she said. 'You'll have to watch that.
Big noses aren't attractive.'

I swatted at her and told her to go away.

'Do you want to race to school?' she
asked. 'It's been a while since we saw who
was faster.'

'You always beat me, Portia,' I said.

'Maybe things have changed.'

'I doubt it,' I replied. 'I'm still the same old Persephone River Pinchgut I've always been and you're still the same annoying old Portia Flame Pinchgut you've always been. No matter what age we are, we'll always be the same people.'

'That's not necessarily true,' Portia said, as she picked up my hairbrush and started brushing my hair.

She hasn't done that since we were little. I'd forgotten how much I liked it. It made me relaxed and sleepy. While she brushed my hair she asked me what I thought about having a new brother or sister.

I've wondered about this since Dad came home. I still can't decide how I feel.

I'm so used to it being just Portia and me. I know I complain about her (with good reason), but I wouldn't be without her for a millisecond. We 'share a special bond', or so everyone keeps telling us. Only twins know what it's like to be twins. Now we're facing the prospect of having another SIBLING. It's a strange thought to take on board when you're ten, almost eleven.

I didn't tell Portia all of this. I didn't have to. She took one look at my face and knew how I felt because:

    a) We can always read each other; and

    b) It was how she was feeling too. I knew that by looking at her.

We hugged and had a little cry together, and then a laugh. Then we hugged again and came out of the bathroom. We didn't say anything to anyone because we didn't need to as we'd already shared it with each other.

# Friday 21 May. 12:48 pm.

Locked in the toilet at school.

I don't normally bring my diary to school, but 'desperate times call for desperate measures', as Gran would say. Our place is a madhouse at the moment. There are far too many people living in it, which means I don't get nearly enough writing time.

The good thing is that Mum and Eleanor are getting on well. I think Mum feels sorry for Eleanor because she is expecting a baby and has no money and is so far away from home. She took her op-shopping for baby things yesterday and she's teaching her pre-natal yoga. That's yoga for pregnant women. Eleanor says it's helping her relax.

Dad is being super helpful around the house. He even made Portia's and my lunch today. It's totally fantastic having him back. When we opened our lunchboxes we discovered we didn't have rye or wholegrain bread, but delicious,

fluffy, yummy white bread sandwiches!

Portia cheered and gave me a high five. 'Yay! White bread!'

Then we did a little dance of joy.

You can tell we don't often get white bread!

BTW, Miss Squirrel-Smith showed us some photos that Mr Cleaver sent to us from Papua New Guinea. He looks very happy in all the shots, which show him helping to build the library, receiving boxes of donated books and working with children in the classroom. One day I hope I can do something worthwhile like Mr Cleaver.

# Saturday 22 May. 11:07 am.

Camping, in Will's tent.

Well, we are here, camping by the river and 'getting back to nature'. It really feels like we're out in the wilderness. There isn't much around except trees, trees and more trees. Oh, and animals.

When we got here, Portia looked around at the magpies and wallabies (grazing contentedly nearby and looking very cute) and shuddered. 'Gross,' she said. 'There are animals everywhere.'

I said it was great.

Portia turned on me. She said it wasn't great, and that camping was hideous. 'What if they attack us, Perse, have you thought of that?'

I was trying hard not to laugh. Then I saw the look on Portia's face and she was totally serious. She's obviously super, super scared of animals.

Gotta go. Mr Divine, I mean Will, popped his head into the tent and asked us to go for a hike with him.

TTFN.

# Sunday 23 May. 12:22 pm.

Soaking up the fresh air by the river.

The hike was lots of fun. Will knows loads about native plants and basically gave us a guided tour through the forest as we went. Portia whinged the whole way. Mum got three leeches down her socks, but she didn't complain. I had my salt handy so we made short work of those squirmy little critters.

Last night we found a baby possum lying on the ground, looking stunned.

I went to pick it up with my jumper when Portia screamed, 'Rat! Rat!' and tried to swat it with a rolled-up cake decoration magazine (which, incidentally, she was trying to get Will to notice earlier, without any luck).

'Don't!' I cried, stopping her just in time.

Will explained in a slow voice – as if he didn't think Portia would understand otherwise – that it was a baby possum.

'Are you sure?' Portia asked. 'It looks like a rat to me.'

'Very sure,' Will insisted.

I asked if we should take the possum to the vet. Will said the possum was fine, and that it was just in shock from falling out of the tree and being attacked by Portia.

While Portia protested that she hadn't actually attacked the possum, Will picked it up with his bare hands and helped it into a tree.

After that, we sat by the campfire and told each other spooky stories. Will has the best ghost stories. Plus, he knows all the constellations so he pointed them out to us.

Portia kept yawning the whole time, but I found it interesting.

She kept throwing me SECRET SIGNALS that said, 'This is boring,' and 'Get a load of this guy,' but I ignored her.

I like Will. I don't mind camping, either.

Mum said she has enjoyed herself, too, although I think we're all looking forward to a hot shower when we get home.

Note to self: make sure I'm the first one in the door, otherwise Portia will hog the bathroom for hours.

# Monday 24 May. 6:53 am.

Lying on my bed.

I'm so excited! Only five more sleeps until our birthday. Bring it on, I say. I wish I didn't have to go to school today. My legs are still aching from my weekend of hiking. I wonder if Mum will let me stay home.

# Monday 24 May. 8:22 am.

Still on my bed.

Nope, Mum won't let me stay home. She says she has far too much work to do for me to be hanging around. Drat.

I asked Portia what she was doing about the *Delicious Intent* cake she so desperately wanted. She hasn't been able to convince Mum or Will to buy it.

Of course, she is moping about this. Typical Portia.

Tuesday 25 May. 4:44 pm.

On the back porch.

Poor Dill, he's trying so hard to win Portia over. He desperately wants her to like him. He brought her over some more of his mum's homemade ice-cream. This time it was toffee and pineapple. Funny combination, I know, but it tastes better than it sounds.

As usual, Portia barely noticed Dill. When he left, I asked her what her problem was.

She shrugged. 'He's a boy.'

I tried telling her that boys aren't so bad and that, sure, Dill was annoying sometimes, but he's still a good kid.

'Yes, and he's still a boy,' she insisted. 'I just don't get them. You know, it's you and me and Mum and our girlfriends. I don't have much to do with boys, especially small smelly ones who throw their underwear at me.'

I pointed out that it wouldn't kill her to be nice to Dill, especially since he is our neighbour.

Portia shrugged and said, 'Treat 'em mean, keep 'em keen.'

I asked her if Cleo taught her that. She said no.

Eleanor was sitting with us in the lounge room at the time and she said quietly, 'He who sows courtesy reaps friendship. He who plants kindness gathers love.'

Portia stared at her for a minute. I

thought she would say something horrible in reply, but she didn't. She just blushed, coughed and then shuffled out of the room.

I asked Eleanor where she got the quote from. She couldn't remember, but she thought it was a good one. I thought so too. I hope Portia remembers it next time Dill comes over.

'Do you want to feel the baby kick?' Eleanor asked suddenly.

I wasn't sure if I did, but I didn't want to be rude so I said, 'Sure.'

She placed my hand on her belly. I felt something tapping.

'Wow, it's busy in there,' I said. 'Are you sure you're only having one baby?'

Eleanor laughed and said she hoped

so. 'We couldn't afford ultrasounds back home, not while the business was going under, so I've assumed it's only one baby. I don't think I could manage twins.'

Trying not to be offended, I asked her what was wrong with twins.

Eleanor hurriedly said twins were a blessing, but that she wasn't up to it.

She said she wasn't like Mum, who she considered to be a dynamo and a way better mother than she would ever be. The fact that she said that was sweet, and sad at the same time.

# Wednesday 26 May. 4:00 pm.

Sitting at my desk.

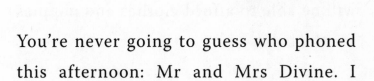

You're never going to guess who phoned this afternoon: Mr and Mrs Divine. I mean Will's parents, Alice and Trevor.

They want to get to know us better, and because Portia and my birthday is coming up they offered to take us out tonight for pizza and a movie.

Wonder of wonders, Mum said yes even though it's a school night.

Can you believe it? Bonus! I'll fill you in on the details when we get home.

Before I go, I must mention that Dad has a new job. It's nothing glamorous. He's working in a software company doing their accounts. It's a start, he says. Mum and Eleanor both breathed a sigh of relief. I think everyone is relieved they will be able to afford clothes and nappies for the baby.

# Wednesday 26 May. 9:52 pm.

Tucked up in bed, ready to doze off.

We got home a little while ago. I had a fantabulous night! Alice and Trevor are like the grandparents we never had (no offence, Gran). They were such fun. They took us to this fabulous pizza restaurant and because they know the owner we got special treatment. We had garlic bread, garlic prawns and pepperoni pizza. We even had creaming soda – and it wasn't sugar-free either.

It was totally the best night. However, I did brush my teeth twice before coming to bed because my breath smells super garlicky.

Alice and Trevor were so nice. They even invited Dill to come with us because he was here when they arrived. He was hanging out and trying to get Portia's attention, as usual.

Portia grumbled at the inclusion of Dill, but not so loud that Alice and Trevor could hear because she's trying to make a good impression on them. I think she still has hopes of moving into their PALACE.

Alice and Trevor drove us to dinner in their GOLD car. I don't remember what type of car it was except that it was super luxurious and expensive-looking. It even had leather seats and cup holders!

We had the best time and I hope we can go out with them again.

Portia spent plenty of time telling Alice

and Trevor about the DILEMMA OF OUR
CAKE. She even brought along her cake
decoration magazine. Can you believe it?

I hope A & T don't feel like they have
to do anything about it. Just because they
look like they're made of money (CA-
CHING!) it doesn't mean they should have
to buy a three-figure-sum cake for Portia

when she spins them her sad little cake-less story.

Honestly, I think our lives have been taken over by cake.

Friday 28 May. 3:47 pm.
In my room.

Because Gran is still in Costa Rica, she's going to miss our birthday party tomorrow (obviously). However a package arrived in the mail today addressed to Portia and me. When we opened the bag there were two identical presents from Gran inside. Gran always gives us the same thing.

I like to wait until my birthday before I open my presents. Of course, Portia is entirely incapable of waiting for anything and had to open hers on the spot.

Typical Portia.

So, without even opening my present I know what I'm getting. A rainbow knitted scarf and matching winter gloves. They are lovely though.

Dill came over again this afternoon trying to impress Portia. She was nearly nice to him. (I think he's wearing her down). That is, until he asked if he could come to the sleepover party.

To which Portia replied, 'Definitely not. It's girls only,' before stomping off.

Poor Dill looked so sad.

'Are you okay? Do you want to play

Monopoly or checkers?' I asked, hoping to cheer him up.

Dill shook his head. 'You like me, Perse-Portia. Why can't the other one?'

I guess he still hasn't got the hang of our names.

I asked him why it mattered so much to him. He said it was because he didn't have any brothers or sisters of his own and that Portia and I could be like sisters to him, if only Portia would be nice to him. He asked me what he'd done to Portia to make her not like him.

'Nothing,' I said. 'Portia is ... different.'

'You're right about that,' Dill said. Then, after a minute, he said, 'Hey, I think I will play Monopoly.'

So we spent the next two hours buying

and selling houses and hotels and I let Dill win so he would feel better.

One more sleep. The best day of the year is almost here.

## Saturday 29 May. 5:51 am.

In bed, under the covers.

Happy birthday to me! Happy birthday to me!

I'm eleven today. It's so exciting! Even Portia is awake and unable to sleep in on our special day. I wonder if it's too early to go and bother Mum and Dad and start opening presents?

Portia thinks not, so off we go.

Back soon.

# Saturday 29 May. 7:02 am.

On the back porch.

I absolutely love what Mum and Portia gave me for my birthday.

Can you guess what it is?

Let me just say, it wasn't on my Birthday Wish List.

It was ... drum roll please ... a goldfish!

I got a goldfish for my birthday!

True, it's not quite a kitten, well nothing like a kitten, but goldfish are low maintenance and Mum considers it a good start to learning how to look after pets.

I have a pet. I finally have a pet!

Apparently, Will would like a kitten or a puppy too (so Mum tells me), but that's way down the track. I'm sure the two of us will eventually wear Mum down.

For now, I have to be content with my goldfish.

The only problem is, I can't think of a name for him. I do have a list of possibilities though.

Top Ten
Fish Names

1. Shorty
2. Fish-Fish
3. Finn
4. Gill
5. Bubbles
6. George
7. Hubert
8. Cleo
9. Goldy
10. Rambo.

I don't think we're quite there yet.

If only I could narrow it down to one good name. Or maybe I should go with all ten, so his name would be Shorty Fish-Fish Finn Gill Bubbles George Hubert Cleo Goldy Rambo.

I've heard of kids being christened with ten or even twenty names. They must have even weirder parents than Portia and me. If that's possible.

# EIGHT FAST FACTS ABOUT GOLDFISH

1. The oldest-ever recorded goldfish was forty-nine years old.

2. They have a memory that lasts up to three months.

3. Goldfish don't have stomachs.

4. They've been trained in synchronised swimming.

5. Goldfish can recognise different human voices and faces.

6. They're the most popular pets in the world.

7. Goldfish are cold-blooded.

8. Goldfish can't close their eyes.

163

Dad didn't have much money to buy Portia and me a present so he got us a card each that includes a birthday IOU. This is what it looks like:

This birthday IOU entitles the bearer, Persephone River Pinchgut, to one year's worth of hugs from her dad, Pickford Pinchgut, plus an ice-cream of her choice at Iggy's Ice-Creamery on her birthday weekend.

I thought that was sweet – and not just because it included ice-cream.

## Saturday 29 May. 12:52 pm.

On the back porch, in the hammock. Just over three hours
until the PRINCESS PARTY
starts.

I like Alice and Trevor. How could I not
after what they did?

We were sitting here having a quiet
birthday lunch with Mum, Dad, Will
and Eleanor before the onslaught of the
PRINCESS PARTY when the doorbell
rings and who should walk in but Alice
and Trevor.

Each of them was carrying a large,
heavy-looking tray with something on
it. I looked, and then looked again.

They were cakes!

Mum saw Portia and me staring and gave us a self-satisfied SECRET SIGNAL. She knew all along and had obviously been planning something with Alice and Trevor while keeping Portia and me in the dark.

One cake was a princess in a pink ball gown with a real doll standing up in it.

The other cake was – and you'll never guess this so I'll just tell you – the Egyptian pharaoh, Tutankhamen. It was for me, obviously. It was the most amazing cake

I'd ever seen, with gold leaf and blue icing and even two cobras sculpted at the top of the headpiece like you see in books.

When Portia saw her cake she squealed and jumped up and down, clapping her hands. 'This is fantastic,' she said over and over.

I, on the other hand, was speechless.

'Do you like your cake, Perse?' Alice asked.

I nodded so hard I thought my head would fall off. 'How did you know?'

Alice laughed. 'Well, Portia did give us a few hints about what you both like.' Then she winked at Portia, who at least had the decency to blush.

'We wanted to get you girls something special for your birthday,' Alice said. 'We thought these cakes might fit the bill. What do you think?'

I said I loved it, and then asked how she made it because it was super clever.

Alice said moulding icing wasn't that different to moulding clay. 'It was a piece of cake, really.'

We all had a giggle at that.

Those cakes sure are incredible. They are way better than anything un-Sunny at *Delicious Intent* could make.

I can't wait until the girls see them. They are going to love, love, love them.

# Saturday 29 May. 9:17 pm.

In the hospital waiting room.

I know you're probably dying to ask why I am sitting in a hospital waiting room. Well, there is an excellent explanation for that.

Here it is.

Our PRINCESS PARTY got underway, as planned, at four o'clock this afternoon with our guests – Jolie, Caitlin, Hayley and Charlotte – arriving. We got great presents, including new purple gel pens for me and a pair of sparkle shoes for Portia, which she's wearing right now. They are indeed very sparkly.

However, I must say that Portia was

rather naughty and invited quite a few more people than she was allowed to. Now I know why she took so long to print those invitations, and why she disappeared at school that time and came back covered in pink and purple ink.

She said she couldn't resist inviting thirty-two other girls to the party.

Thirty-two!!!!

Mum was furious. But it wasn't like she could send the girls home when they arrived dressed in their prettiest party outfits with their parents smiling and asking when they could be picked up.

While Will went out for extra food supplies, Mum told Portia that she would be having extremely stern words with her once the party was over and that a three-month

stint of time-out in her bedroom would be coming up. It's kind of like jail for an eleven-year-old.

For two whole hours we partied, ate loads of yummy food (including our superb cakes, which everyone ADORED), danced and played charades and other games.

Mum, Will, Dad, Eleanor, Alice and Trevor (who stayed on for the party) were busy making sure us girls were happy and having fun. It must have been too much for Eleanor because she went pale again and started getting pains in her stomach and Mum said it was time for her baby to come.

Right there at the party!

Mum, Will and Dad cleared out the party guests quickly. Even Jolie, Caitlin,

Hayley and Charlotte had to go home. They didn't mind. They said our PRINCESS PARTY with the super-duper delicious decorated cakes was the best party ever, even though they couldn't sleep over as planned. They totally understood that we wanted to go to hospital with Dad and Eleanor to welcome our new brother or sister into the world.

But then things got complicated.

Oh, gotta go! Dad's back, looking exhausted but excited. I wonder what he's got to say.

# Saturday 29 May. 9:29 pm.

Hospital waiting room

continued ...

Wow. I can hardly write because my hand is shaking so much.

I mentioned before that things were complicated. That was because when we arrived at the hospital, all eight of us, the doctors pretty quickly found out that Eleanor wasn't going to have one baby. They examined her and said she was having two. Babies, I mean.

Twins.

Like Portia and me.

It gets better – and more complicated.

Dad just came to tell us that Eleanor has

had the babies and that they're all okay.

However, there aren't two babies.

There are three.

Three identical babies.

Three identical boy babies.

Triplets!

Apparently the odds of that happening are totally tiny.

Nevertheless, it has happened.

Our family just grew.

By a lot.

In one hit.

How am I supposed to cope with that?

A thought has just occurred to me. Now I don't only have to share my birthday with a sister, now I have to share my birthday with three brothers too.

Gee, and here I was thinking I was special.

# Saturday 29 May. 11:41 pm.

Tucked up in bed. Last entry tonight, I promise.

Yawn! We're finally home from the hospital. What an amazing day it's been.

We got to see our baby brothers for the first time. They are tiny, and they're being kept in clear plastic container-thingies called 'humidicribs' to help them grow and develop properly. But the doctors said they are healthy and well.

I can't wait to hold them. There is so much I want to tell them and teach them. The number one fact being that their cool sister is called Perse and their bossy sister is called Portia. That's something they will learn pretty quickly for themselves, I'm sure.

I've never seen so many grown adults cry as I did tonight when everyone saw those babies. Luckily, they were tears of joy, not tears of sadness. Portia and I shared a few tears too, plus a few SECRET SIGNALS of 'Isn't this awesome!' and 'What the heck will we do with so many brothers?'

'I wish I'd been nicer to Dill now,' Portia whispered to me. 'I could have practised on him before these guys came along.'

'It's never too late to try to be nice, Portia,' I said.

Portia smiled and said that from now on she'd try to understand boys more.

I told her she would have to, especially since we would all be living in our tiny house.

You may be wondering what names Dad and Eleanor came up with for the boys. It didn't take them long. They were much quicker than I have been at choosing a name for my goldfish, which I still haven't done. Here they are:

FRASER LIAM PINCHGUT
BOURKE OLIVER PINCHGUT
REAGAN SCOUT PINCHGUT

Good, solid names, don't you think?

When we got home, there were fireworks lighting up the sky. Portia was convinced they were for our birthday. I'm certain they weren't, but it was a nice way to end an eventful eleventh birthday.

# Sunday 30 May. 9:17 am.

On the back porch, trying to soak up
the weak autumn sun.

I still can't believe I have three brothers!
Mum and Dad are taking us to see them
again later today, as soon as visiting hours
start at the hospital. I can't wait.

We're also going to cash in our birthday
IOU voucher that Dad gave us for Iggy's
Ice-creamery. Yum!

Firstly, though, there are a few more
news items I need to share with you before
I reach the last page of this diary, which
is very close.

Alice and Trevor dropped by this
morning with Will. They sat us all down at

the kitchen table and said that they didn't think we should continue to live in this tiny house, and that Dad and Eleanor and the triplets couldn't be expected to share one room.

This wasn't news to me. I'd heard Mum and Will talking about this in the car ride home last night. Plus, the studio is now full because the boxes that Portia and I saw when we Skyped Dad while he was still in England arrived on our doorstep the other day!

While Mum and Will didn't seem to be able to come up with a solution to our space problem, it seems Alice and Trevor have.

They said they were old and lonely and didn't want Will to move out of their gigantic house. They also said they had enjoyed getting to know Portia and me. (Who would have thought?)

'Will you make our lives a little richer and a little warmer by coming and living with us?' Trevor asked us.

Alice added, 'All of you. We love babies, Pickton, though we never had many of our own. Plus, we'd like to help you out, too, so we can all be one big happy family together. What do you say?'

Before anyone could reply, Portia started jumping up and down and chanting, 'Yes! Yes! Yes!'

'I'm not sure,' Mum said. 'We'd hate to impose.'

Dad seemed to be in shock. 'All of us?' he asked. 'Well, that is generous of you.'

Portia continued to jump up and down

and chant, 'We're going to live in a palace. We're going to live in a palace.'

Alice and Trevor insisted that we should all go and live with them. From what I saw the other day there is definitely room for everyone. We could probably fit another three families in, actually.

Will squeezed Mum's hand. Mum looked at Dad who shrugged and said he thought we could give it a go. He said he'd work around the house and help out doing whatever he could, whenever he could.

Mum offered to look after the gardens and give Alice and Trevor as many yoga and laughter therapy sessions as they wanted.

'We can sort that out later,' Alice said. 'What we really want is to enjoy the sound of children's laughter again.'

Trevor smiled in agreement.

'What about Portia's moaning?' I said. 'That's not a sound you want to hear.'

Everyone laughed at that, except Portia, who tried to whack me.

'Just think, girls, you could finally have your own rooms,' Mum said. 'No more arguments.'

Portia and I looked at each other and both said at exactly the same time, 'No way! We'll still share no matter what.' Then we giggled and hugged each other and all the adults hugged each other too.

Oh boy, what are we getting ourselves into?

I sure hope I get a turret room. I've always wanted a round bedroom.

The second and last announcement

I have for you, at least in this diary, is that Mrs Pickleton dropped her own BOMBSHELL this morning. She and Dill dropped by to see if they could help with anything and Mum told them we were moving.

This made Mrs Pickleton and Dill sad, but we promised we would visit often and told them that they would always be welcome at the PALACE.

Dill was looking mopey. When I asked why he said he really wanted a baby brother or sister. We now had three, which he thought was unfair.

Just then Mrs Pickleton broke into the biggest grin ever and said, 'You know what? I might be able to help you with that.'

Super curious, we all asked what she

meant. She laughed and blushed and said that she was having a baby. Finally. After trying for years.

Dill squealed, 'I've waited my whole life for this. Do you really mean it?'

Mrs Pickleton nodded and said she really meant it.

Then everyone squealed and handed out hugs and kisses left, right and centre because we were so happy for Mrs Pickleton and Dill. They were both finally getting what they really, really wanted.

So, I guess this diary hasn't been so much a birthday bonanza, but rather a BABY BONANZA. Funny the way things turn out.

I have to sign off now because I'm out of pages. Hopefully, it won't be long before I'm back with a fantabulous new adventure.

Oh, I forgot to mention. I finally decided on a name for my goldfish. It's Marmalade. I hope you like it! That reminds me, he's due for a feed.

Until next time, TTFN.

_Aleesah_

Hi, I'm Aleesah, the author of this book.

I grew up in the country and had a lot of freedom as a nine-year-old. My older brother, my cousin and I would ride our bikes and go exploring, build cubbyhouses and billycarts, and rescue injured animals and birds. When I wasn't outdoors, I was usually curled up on my bed reading. It was quite an addiction for me and I often got into trouble for 'having my nose in a book'. I loved colouring in and won loads of prizes for my efforts. Quite shockingly, I also loved school!

I wrote stacks of stories and illustrated them with crazy stick figures. Like Perse, I kept a diary. And I can always remember desperately wishing I had an identical twin.

Serena

Hi, I'm Serena, the illustrator of this book.

I don't really look this freaky, but as an artist, I can make myself look as kooky as I like, and you need to be able to laugh at yourself sometimes.

I grew up in Melbourne with an older brother who taught me how to wrestle, an older sister who always had the coolest clothes and jewellery and a younger sister who enjoyed following me around everywhere!

I loved drawing, writing notes in my diary, dressing up our pet cat in dolls' clothes and creating mini adventures in our huge backyard. When I was nine years old, long socks were really cool, funny dresses with lots of frills and buttons were cool, straight hair was cool and even big teeth were cool... unfortunately I was not cool.

# Other titles in the Totally Twins series.

www.totallytwins.com.au